MW01535967

Eternal Bliss

– My Journey to the Divine

Vrinda Bhatnagar

BlueRose ONE
Stories Matter

First Published in June 2022

ISBN: 978-93-5628-561-3

BLUEROSE PUBLISHERS
www.BlueRoseONE.com
info@bluerosepublishers.com
+91 8882 898 898

Cover Design:
Aveek

Typographic Design:
Rohit

Distributed by: BlueRose, Amazon, Flipkart

Dedication

This book is dedicated to my father,

Late Sh. Anil Bhatnagar

Love.

We are living in a society characterized by the cultural plurality of high modernity, increasing anxiety, hyper competition, rampant consumerism, dislocated families and sharing economy. What does this mean in social context for spirituality of my generation (Gen Z)? This question always keeps us baffled – what's the purpose of our life, who are we? These are never taught in our so called modern education system! This book has answers to that with real life experiences of the author.

This book originally stemmed from the author's deep devotion for Krishna-The dark-hued God, her multiple visits to Vrindavan, her spiritual upbringing and a series of events that happened in this journey. She always accepted it as Lord's higher plan. In this book, she discussed both her life experiences and how they changed her. You will find stories and experiences that will help you increase your faith in God. It's not a book but the author's spiritual journey - what she learned, how she felt, and insights into real life situations gained through the writing.

Back in the olden days of the 80s and 90s, there was no WhatsApp. Telegram has reincarnated to a new avatar (App). Old telegram is no more! There was no daily instant messaging. There was no requirement to answer within a split second, nor was there the expectation to read and respond after each message. It just wasn't a thing. Back then, it was about letters and handwriting. It's a historical thing for my generation. In this book, the author will introduce to you a few high impact letters from 90s with timeless wisdom.

Don't miss ManasikYatra (the mesmerizing virtual trip) to Vrindavan, Barsana and picturesque landscapes of VrajDham along with the author in the early chapters.

The exploration journey continued when she started reading His Divine Grace Srila Prabhupada's books. She got solid foundation of who Krishna is, His pastimes, what's Karma, What's real essence of love, etc.

Starting off as a kid Vrinda, by reading the Bhagavad Gita "As it is" to writing this book, which took her closer to the Lord has been the most beautiful journey. A cruise filled with questions and answers, revelations and desires, a quest that gradually answered all her questions on love and life. This spiritual awakening in her has been covered towards the last chapters of the book.

Let us go forward together with open minds and good hearts as we further take part in our life's journey with Bhagavad Gita. This book will definitely catalyze and inspire one to read Bhagavad Gita "As it is." This masterpiece by Vrinda can be appreciated in many ways Congratulations to the author once again. I am glad now to terminate this foreword and allow the readers to get on with the joy of reading.

-Your Aspiring Servant

Achyut Hari Prabhu

Acknowledgement

This book wouldn't have been possible without the constant support of my mother, Mrs. Anupam. The encouragement my mother and my grandfather, Dr. P.K. Bhatnagar have given me throughout my journey is unparalleled. I really want to thank my constant, who put up with me during this journey of mine, Mahika. I would like to extend my heartfelt appreciation and gratitude for the support I have received from Shri Achyut Hari Prabhuji, Mrs. Madhulika Neville and Shri Govind Krsna Das who have all helped me get closer to my understanding of the dark-hued Krishna.

I would also like to thank all my friends who have made it possible for me to bring my dreams onto paper in the form of this book.

Lastly, I want to thank my publishers, Blue Rose Publishers for bringing my dreams to reality and giving me a platform.

I arrived at the land of the mysterious, the land of the makkanchor, the thief who stole not just butter but also the hearts of many. I could hear the ringing of the bells and people calling out 'Radhey Radhey'.

As I walked along the land of the chit chor, I left my heart with someone called Radha. As I walked along the shores of the Yamuna, I saw a little bit of him and a little bit of her.

A calmness in her voice and love in her heart
Many people may not know who she is.
A different light on her face
And glitter in her flight
Many people may not know her name
It is her that brightens the day.
They worship her, they sing her name aloud
But she shall be found in the heart

The heart of the dense forest where he resides.
They played and danced on those river banks,
They loved in the nikunjas
But it is her that they might not know about.
She is no mystery to me but yet I cannot tell you how.
From years on end she comes to the streets
Looking for her beloved, oh Krishna.
Her name on my lips and automatically his name conjoins
I know Him through dear kishori
But you might know madhav before
I found my heart with her.
She has many names,
But the dearest to her; Radhey
That is what I call her
I look for Her on the banks of Yamuna
And the temples I visit.
It is Radhe that you might not understand
But it is all that I understand, Radhe.

Books are the basis; purity is the force; preaching is the essence; utility is the principle.

-A. C. Bhaktivedanta Swami Prabhupada

Contents

ONE

The concrete to

my road

"You are here to enable the divine purpose of the Universe to unfold. That is how important you are!"

— Eckhart Tolle

Looking at the cover, a lot of you would simply assume that this book is full of religious connotations, but let me tell you this; it is NOT. I was born in the year 2000 in a very religious family, and I was very happy, I still am. But during my early childhood, I never really understood what bhakti (devotion) is and why my father is so attached to Krishna. It took me more than a decade to pick up some of his old books, and while going through tons of his email exchanges between him and so many other people, I decided to follow the path of my father but with questions in my mind and a path I had to pave on my own. This is about a Y-generation kid trying to find answers and seemingly getting more and more emotionally involved in what I am going to share with you next. Now, before this question arises within your minds as to why am I writing a book on my journey and why you should read it, well, a very simple answer to that is, I do not know, and I might never have the answer to that question but I can just tell you that maybe there is a slight possibility that this might lead you on a similar path as me or you could understand me.

So yes, getting back to what I am writing about, well, I had just started reading the Bhagavat Gita and I was mesmerized. I did hear it ample number of times that this book is the way of life and it gives you the answers to every possible question you might have. I started reading it and with time passing by, I started getting the proposition, the reasons behind every word said in this amazing book, Gita. I am definitely not a saint. I am just an ordinary twenty-year-old, who maybe lives around the block. I had questions arising at every given point in this little journey that I had set up for myself, and I didn't have much trust on the fact that I might actually understand anything, given the reason I never really understood why my father was so involved. From time to time, people helped me overcome these doubts and I finished reading the Bhagavat Gita. This was the foremost step that I took to pave my way through.

These weary debates about what is written in the book with my grandfather were like evening tea to us, loved by all but way too hot. These debates not only cleared our various doubts, but also brought me a little closer to climbing the next step on the ladder called bhakti (devotion). Generally, a girl my age would tell you how amazing it is to party and go out with friends, I probably would have said the same a while ago, but now you would spot me all cuddled up in a corner, completely engrossed and mesmerized with any sort of book on bhakti (devotion). This idea of devotion perplexed me but what baffled me the most is the idea, the mere thought of pure, true love. Putting words like pure and true together with the word love sounds strange doesn't it? It is strange because a feeling that is already pious like true love is so pure that it does not need to be proved or reverenced. Mentioning this sentence adds a little more confusion as to why I said what I said. Well, because the purest form of love is devotion, which, in today's world, is not understood by many. Moreover, it is something a lot of people look down upon. Love is so rare that we barely see it around ourselves, and look at me, lost in my own thoughts; I continued this little journey to eventually find myself exploring love. Many of us do not realize that what we call love today is just proclivity, just an inclination towards a particular thing. What happens when we humans find a different object or human to latch onto? We name that love as well.

I did not exactly have a wonderful childhood and a big reason for that is my own stupidity and abrupt interpretation of the Y-generation love stories that we all so blindly believe in by looking at a couple of movies where the train is always almost missed and the hero saves the heroine. Well, I set out to mark my path and find virtue in this play called 'life'. This whole idea of love and life that we carry with ourselves, comparing our lives to that of certain movie characters, really derails us from the truth of our existence.

With everything so westernized in our lifestyle, it was quite a journey that I had decided to sway away with. The lifestyle we have is so easily adapted to and growing more of techno-savvy with each passing day that we almost forget the whole purpose of our lives. It is way too young to embark upon a journey, a quest to find ourselves, isn't it? Well, that is what I also thought, but with each passing moment, I had a different question as well as a different fear in my mind.

The first fear that settled deep into my mind was 'what would people say? Am I too young to be talking like this? Am I of the correct age to ask the questions hovering around like bees?' Then I realized that this whole notion of what is the correct age for bhakti is set deep inside in all of us by the society. I have also heard it a lot of times from my peers and various other sources of contact, exclaiming the moment I said the word bhakti, "Is this not for old people? Children and adults should enjoy their lives. This idea of who is of the appropriate age to offer them unto the supreme godhead baffled me. I was quite certain that rules like these are not applied on us by Shri Krishna himself, rather it is just an excuse made up by people to continue living their life as per the westernized society.

After realizing that this is just a mere excuse, I continued my quest to find answers to my questions. With the first fear out of my mind, I could feel myself more drawn, more indulged in the Supreme personality. Well, let me give you a bit of a backstory. So, probably rewinding my life about a decade and a half ago, as I mentioned above that my family has always been very religious, especially my father. I felt that for my father, it was more than just a religion. It was something connected to the deep roots of his soul; he used to get immense pleasure by just taking the name of the Godhead. Every night, before going to bed, he used to read me stories of Krishna. To me, they were just any random bedtime stories, which I assumed would be heard by a lot of other kids as well. Time passed by and the reading of these stories grew from daily routines into monthly sankirtan (call and response chanting) groups and bi-weekly visits to the Vrindavan dham. I was just too young to find myself in any of those practices. To me, it was an activity done because of my parents. You know how it is like when a young child is approximately of the age of five, they do what their parents do. They tend to copy the life of the parents in order to feel more important and probably more authoritative; well, that is exactly why I most certainly played along. It was not a choice I had made for myself. Whilst I was deeply submerged in my thoughts to better understand why I was born in this particular family, a shloka (verse) from the Bhagavat Gita dawned upon me. In the sixth chapter of the book, in the 41stshloka (verse):

Prapyapunya-krtamlokan

Usitvasasvatihsamah

Sucinamsrimatamgehe

Yoga-bhrastobhijayate

This means - the unsuccessful yogi, after many years of enjoyment on the planet of the pious living entities, is born into a family of righteous people, or into a family of rich aristocracy.

With growing minutes on my clock I started to realize that these were the choices I once made, maybe not right now, maybe not even a hundred years ago, but these were some choices that I made for myself, that from the very beginning of my mortal life, I was bestowed upon the happiness that I could be born in a family where bhakti was already prevalent, where I would have some sort of guiding light at every given step of my life to understand more and more as to why I was born in such a family. They say that your Punyakaram (good deeds) bring you closer to Krishna and this was Krishna's way of bringing me closer to himself. Getting back to the present day, with these certain questions already answered, I was ready to take the next step. I then decided to find the answer to the question 'who is Krishna?' Before I started this journey, he was a god to me, supreme god, but what that meant still eluded me. I always heard his name in my household but I could never grasp as to who he actually is. It is very important to ask questions; blindly believing in anything does no good to any soul because if all the doubts are not cleared we cannot take the step with full faith, with utmost confidence. As Krishna says, "who seeking knowledge will gain knowledge."

TWO

The letter

To write is human, to receive a letter: Divine!
Susan Lendroth

One does not attain this knowledge in the blink of an eye, for some, it takes various reincarnations as well. It is not a very difficult path to walk upon, although making up your mind that this is what you want for the rest of your life is the hard part. We live in a world where commitment has very less value; most people run away from this word so to commit to Krishna seems like an even greater deal as rather than loving godhead, people fear them. We think about repercussions as we live in a world where we might do bad things and not feel an ounce of guilt but we get easily scared with the idea of ending in hell after leaving the mortal world.

With this, the second fear silently crept into my heart and it was so difficult to overcome as it involved the polluted feeling of selfishness. Now, everybody might say that we are very kind and we are not selfish at all but deep down, every single person has a motive, a personal agenda to do what they do. People tend to look for a favorable outcome and to achieve that outcome, they make certain selfish decisions as well. This feeling is something that only brings kingdoms down, like an enemy of the soul. Well, I was basically stupid when I started this journey. Therefore, being the typical millennial kid, I started a foolish barter system with Krishna. The whole idea behind this was to receive favorable outcomes, which was fairly selfish of me. I asked him for materialistic things in return of my bhakti, and as I tried the good old system, I could not get any sort of reciprocation, I could not find myself moving forward with either my needs or my demand for the quest to understand love. It frustrated me to a certain point where I assumed that I would never receive any answer to my queries. Time flew by, and I read and read, until I stumbled upon a letter sent to my father years ago by a saint of Vrindavan. With each word that I read, I drowned in my own tears. The letter had no fancy words or huge promises, to the eyes of a layman, it was just another letter. There was nothing really special but each word in that letter had an astonishingly amazing effect on me. The letter was about Barsana, each and every word depicted pure divinity in that. It was just a letter explaining about the land of Barsana, the temples and the surroundings of Barsana. It is the holy land of Shrimati Radharani ji, as beautiful as her name, the place is filled with various temples dedicated to radha-rani and her love for Krishna.

The letter which described about the land of Barsana is mentioned below:

PremSudhaDhara: Anilji
ShriHari
ShriDhaamBarsana
14th September 1990
Dear Anil,
With love, Jai ShriHari.

Seeing the address of ShriDhaam on the envelope, do not assume that we have reached Barsana. We came to the comforting site of ShriShriSwamini (Shri Radha) on eighth morning; carrying the delightful memories of ShriNandgaon. We propose to go to Shri Van on the 17th, which can be implemented with the grace of ShriHari.

The path which leads into the fields and forests and down to the streams of BrajBhoomi is enchanting. It seems that the delights of Paradise are reflected by a cosmic mirror onto the pilgrimage sites here. Snuggling BrajrajKunwar's childhood play in its bosom, Nandgaon attracts countless sentimental devotees till date. It is not only the ground where the lovable pranks and playful dalliances of youthful Krishna (from His fifth to sixteenth year) have taken place and are occurring till date. ShriLalitasar, KrishanKund and dense foliage of the forest endorse these escapades. You cannot see the PaniharinKund and the footprints of ShriCharanh but that does not matter because some eager curiosity will inspire you later on. Similarly, the birthplace of ShriShriSwamini and the area of her childhood are mesmerizing. People like us, who cannot travel much, can see ShriShriji's high bhavan imparting delight. Attended and adorned by dense foliage, it makes us rapturous till date. I was thinking of showing you

Vilasgarhi with its magnificent mountain range, but I was tired those days and time was also scarce. You might have had a glimpse but Aalok and Mudit haven't.

The sacred dhaam of Barsana is not merely a sight of child play. Here also, RasraajNandkunwar, guised in various flashy forms, comes for a rendezvous with the young Kishori of Vrashbhanu. He stops over at times. Gaharvan abounding with these amorous frolics, blossoms radiantly today. Both the passionate kunwar and kishori secretly enjoying themselves; often surrounded by sakhis and sometimes in isolation, are engrossed in several romantic dalliances and spirited antics. The metaphorical search of the impassioned soul, for union with the handsome god is centered within earthly Vrindavana. It is here that we shall find the dark god fluting in the blossoming pastures of His youth. Even though the mundane world has veiled the constant joy; but the forest is still the same today, the sites are the same, these kunjas and nikunjas, the sacred river Yamuna and its sandy banks are just the same. Those who can see the divine play are steeped in it. The temporal plane does not jolt them or deprive them of joy in Vrindavana, which is the source of several playful dalliances of Shri Radha-Krishna. Rasikas (persons moved by passionate religious devotion for Krishna) engrossed in the spirited antics of Krishna on the banks of Kalindi are sighting this divine play till date.

The abundance of romantic dalliances impassions fortunate devotees in Nidhivan. Shri Van, snuggling the child play of Lord Krishna in its bosom, is a storehouse of wealth. Idyllic and sensuous Vrindavana becomes the perfect landscape in which madhurya or the sweet love of Krishna unfolds. The divine peaks of ShriGiriraj, mountain passes, cascading waterfalls, the verdant groves, ponds and lakes; are all the charmingly blessed sites of sakhya rasa (in which the devotee imagines himself as a companion or sakha of the deity) and madhurasa (where Krishna is construed as the bee attracted to various flowers or sakhis); the adorable means of romantic dalliances. I had not planned this write-up but Krishna, the Rasiya, gets precisely what He wants. In reality, a person becomes solely His on knowing Krishna's enigmatic persona. It is here that peacocks dance in ecstasy, birds sing passionately, bees dance around lotus pollen and sing a love song, cranes and swans fly towards and cows are drawn to the call of the flute. We awaken to a world of Vishnu, who resides not only in the hearts of gopis but also in the sap that animates the birds and the bees, the trees and creepers of Vrindavana.

Savoring the closeness with Lord Krishna, absorbed in His love delights us with joyous abandon. In such a case, one does not get attached to the world of apparent reality by doing duties, and is not distanced from union with the divine. The supremely enchanting form of Lord Krishna, with His loving tenderness and the supportive canopy of His shelter does not abandon us even for a second. Adopting the same delightful basis, when we conduct ourselves, the end result is ecstatic. I have the same expectations from you. An indifferently cold attitude, insensitivity, indifference; these entire traits make the mind unemotional and arid; while Rasik Shekhar (title of Krishna) resides in a sentimental persona...so why would His devotees be heartless! We must certainly remember that due to negligence, we do not become attached to those very people and their conduct. Keep the mind under control.

With love,

Yours Bobo.

It was in this moment I had realized that I was not looking for answers, rather I was looking for happiness in tangible things. The biggest fault in a human is to find short-lived happiness, to find material happiness which does not last long. Once that is over, they get super busy in finding happiness in something else. We get trapped in this cycle of life, not understanding that these things, this material happiness can never last. It does not matter how much wealth we accumulate or what we achieve if we do not surrender to Krishna. Grazing the way back to my senses, I asked Krishna to show his mercy on me and continued. At this point, you might realize that I was getting nowhere, which was exactly my thought, because I did not know where to start from. Well, I did reach a small plateau of bhakti, of devotion, because love and devotion are huge mountains which are so high we might never be able to see the peak. It is substantial to understand what the highest peak of that mountain is for you, as a person will receive utmost happiness by fulfilling this journey. For me, my highest peak was Krishna, and even when a person reaches this peak, the highest point of the mountain, the love for Krishna, will never end. Krishna, the supreme personality, omnipresent, was the goal of my journey. This journey was to understand Krishna and I did understand his personality. Living on the mritu-loka (mortal world) we humans often forget the purpose of our lives, that is, to do our duty (dharma) and accept the decisions based on those duties, known as karma. But the most important duty is to serve the godhead shri Krishna himself. We often forget that above and beyond our blue planet, there is a celestial sky, which is eternal, divine, and transcended. Even beyond this beautiful sky is the abode of shri Krishna, goloka. Shri Krishna is the supreme purusha, the indestructible light, and with this new found knowledge about Krishna, I thought I was a know-it-all, so I instantaneously started to exhibit all I could pick together about Krishna. From this, my journey of ahankar (ego) started. Ego binds us in ourselves, leaving us no vacuum to breathe in the room, that ego as well as that void filled up inside of me as I thought that I had already reached my goal, At this particular point, this moment was a lot for me to take in, as at the very beginning of this journey, I had no idea I could prowess so much knowledge. Later, I realized it was an attempt to self-harm that I assumed to know about Krishna so much without even knowing him. My ambitions and appetite did not fulfill my desire to find love in this. I did read about Krishna, I did hear about Krishna but I was yet to understand Krishna as it was not yet my time to dive deeper in this as I was not ready. I decided to take a few steps back and give myself the space and time to process the already existing knowledge of Krishna and the absolute known when I was having such a great difficulty in understanding the basics of how I would dive deeper. I decided to read more; I decided to spend more time on Krishna. The elusive mysteries connected with Krishna intrigue me more and more with each passing day. The world that we reside in is a mayajal as Shakespeare said that "*All the world's a stage*," in which mortals are stuck in this mayajal until Krishna liberates them from this leela.

THREE

Towards the dham

O <u>Brahmā</u>, whatever appears to be of any value, if it is without relation to Me, has no reality. Know it as My illusory energy, that reflection which appears to be in darkness. –

SB2.9.34

This maya-jaal that the humans are stuck in is mere lies and materialistic ambitions that can never be satisfied. But this is a maya-jaal for those who are ignorant of the beautiful creation of the supreme godhead himself. I started to begin my days with a new perspective, immense positivity, and of course, with Krishna's name. As I looked up, the rays of the sun made my eyes shrink, and I looked away. But somehow, and I don't know why, I looked up again, and when I did, the feeling was different. I could feel a sense of wisdom dawn upon me as I tried to get myself up to the par of diving deep in the shyam-kund of my thoughts. With a rosary in my hand, I started chanting the name of Madhava. Once

freed from the maya of life, all mortals start to seek the soul truth, the absolute truth, Madhusudhana.

Like everybody else, I became a seeker of the Paramatama. The satisfaction, the calm us humans are always looking for was later on understood by me to be Krishna himself. Devotion of Shri Krishna is what transcends the mortals into the bhava, prem (love). This realization came upon me in a very later stage of this expedition. During this journey, various fears kept me on my toes. The fear of disappointment is so deep rooted in our hearts that we tire ourselves to prove to the world and to ourselves that we are worthy. We always try to prove that no matter what, we will not disappoint others in any given situation. To be honest, the whole idea behind being disappointed is very scary to us humans as it seems to be an overwhelming emotion. It can either make a person stronger or the person might even lose all their will in the process. To understand the shashwatam (the divine) we have to let go of materialistic greed, but it is not as easy as it seems and is often misunderstood by others.

Letting go of materialistic needs does not in any way or form ask us to leave our dharma (duty) and our karma, as they are the absolutes of our lives. I too was aberrant throughout this journey, just to realize that I was being attached to Krishna. The acrimonious relationships that we sometimes mistake as love often lead us down a very tedious path whereas love for Krishna brings us the utmost joy. With the complete adulation in my heart for Krishna, I kept fighting my inner battles to overcome my fears. Most of these battles were first fought with the outside world, namely toxic relationships.

The twisted game of friendship that has been going around for quite some time has hurt almost every kid of this generation. Friendships? Twisted? Not really, well true friendships are immensely joyful. Friendship, which is supposed to be a bond of pure innocence, trust, and power, has become an adversary these days. And to blame it on anyone else would be wrong. These competitions are so deep-seated that we fail to understand that there is so much more to life than to just compete with our peers. At the very beginning of my quest to find these answers, I was very cantankerous and that was the biggest challenge I had to overcome. The personality traits that I had imbibed and embedded into my soul were very toxic to say the least. Not only did it hurt others around me, it also hindered my progress on a path that I had yet to pave for myself. At this point, a question would arise in your mind as to why I am just going on about what I faced? What were the issues I had? Well, to say the least, the yuga (era) that we all are born in, these personality traits become a person's identity and are present in almost everybody at this point of time. We do not even realize how toxic we are to someone and how the toxic energy of others affects our peace of mind. Therefore, to even go ahead and understand more about the journey, it is very important to wipe away the fog of these traits from our lives to clearly see where we are headed. The divyam (divine) energy, Shri Krishna, is not very hard to reach. It is just about the intentions you call upon him that matter. He is the originator of this brahmand (universe) everything began from him, the other gods were born, and once we surrender ourselves over to him, all toxicity leaves our lives. Everything happening around us is his leela but that is not to be confused by his will. We all are just parts and parcels of the ADI PURUSHA, Bhagavatgita: 4.35

yajjnatvanapunarmoham
evamyasyasipandava
yenabhutanyasesani
draksyasyatmanyathomayi
This simply means that,

"And when you have thus learned the truth, you will know that all living beings are but part of me—and that they are in me, and are mine." Everything happens according to his will but he has given all of us the freedom to choose our own paths. Thereafter, it's up to us to find Krishna through our aantarmann (soul). All the actions that we do directly have an effect on us which might not be realized in the near future but those are not the actions of Krishna, they are our own choices. Getting rid of moh-maya is our duty but Krishna lights up the path for us once we surrender unto him. This is what happened with me as well. Once I decided to find Krishna, the supreme personality, I was ready to get rid of the vikaar (negativities) inside of me to take a leap of faith. Time passed by, and I slowly got rid of the impurities that hampered my thoughts and beliefs, only to finally discover the happiness that was buried deep inside of me. As I started to cogitate more about Shyamsundara, I found myself thinking about him at every point of time. Every conversation of mine consisted of his thoughts and at this point, I realized that I was walking on the right track, on the track that I had not thought of treading on even in my dreams. There is a cornucopia of devotion inside all of us; it is just a matter of a few choices that lead us either in the direction of Krishna or away from him. Once attached to Krishna, the devotee will always have Krishna in his/her heart. A shloka described in the Siksatakam reminds me of love incarnate Shri Chaitanya Mahaprabhu's words:

'yugayitamnimeshenchakchusha-pravrishayitam
Shoonyayitamjagatsarvam,Govindvirhenmey'

This simply means that "oh beloved Krishna! A moment of separation seems like a million years have passed without you. Tears never stop flowing from my eyes. The whole world seems to be blank. There is no charm. Oh Govinda! Your separation leaves me in this state." This is the plight of the devotee who has Krishna deep in their soul. The first realization that you have from Krishna is that Krishna is your friend and mentor. And this is what happened to me as well. I started talking to people who thought alike, those who would serve lord Krishna and the people I could discuss Krishna with. After a long and hard search, I found some peers in my old group of friends who were more than ecstatic to listen to his name and that is where I started seeing Krishna in my friends. Seeing Krishna in other people does not mean that you see his image. It simply means that you start finding more elements of prem (love), loyalty, and various other aspects in relations. Not to say I became choosy, I have always been open to the idea of having new people in my life as each person has something of their own that they can end up teaching us. It is just that after a point, my life started to revolve around Murlidhar. This feeling left me speechless most of the times, because this feeling of understanding is my own worth. Moreover, the worth of different relationships in my life really brought about a change in my personality. Rather than just looking forward to what might be the best solution for me, I started considering the interests of others in my mind as well. There is no greater friendship than that of godhead Krishna and his friend Sudama. Almost everyone must have heard their story, an all-powerful king and his poor friend sudama. The pure bhava of prem, mitrprem (love for friend) is often seen in their friendship. Nothing matters if you accept one as your friend, no wealth in the world changes the feeling of respect towards each other. Throughout this journey, I realized who understood me from a very different perspective. The idea of friendship that we millennials dwell upon is very narcissistic. It burdens us in all ways and forms, and this is not the true essence of friendship at all. With time, as I kept realizing my toxicity, I kept eliminating that as well.

Time passed by and with uncountable visits to Vrindavan dham since my childhood days, when I thought about the place and visited the dham, I could not control my teary eyes. Vrindavan is the abode of shri Krishna on earth. Vrindavan(vrinda ka van) is filled with vrinda plants, commonly known as tulsi plant. The present day Vrindavan with Shri Yamunaji, pilgrimage sites, and idyllic landscape is a temporal reflection of the eternal Vrindavan or golok, where God dwells forever. Shri Naradji says that Lord Krishna dispatched chaurasi, encapsulating Shri Goverdhan and ShriYamunaji to earth. Weaving the leelas or divine play of Shri Krishna, Vrindavan shows us the path of union with the divine.

The Puranas, Sanskrit Texts and devotees have unanimously accepted its significance. Medieval times, with the Krishna cult at its crest, were flooded with rasiks, people with intense devotional love for Krishna; Raskhanand Taaj, inspite of being Muslim devotees, were insanely fond of Vrindavan, with history recounting the good fortune of the Mughal emperor Akbar till date. The highly knowledgeable Shri Uddhavaji reflected that 'so steeped in the love of Krishna are the hearts of the gopis, so pure are their thoughts that while others may only aspire towards the state of oneness with the Lord, these simple cowherdesses have already attained it.' The metaphorical search of the impassioned soul for union with Lord Krishna is centered within earthly Vrindavan or perhaps that region in the heart wherein god is ultimately found. Till date, the divine incarnate Lord Krishna is resplendent in his madhurya form of loving tenderness in Vrindavan. ShriKuresh Swami writes that if we cannot be born as animated beings such as insects, flies, or even grass in Vrindavan, it is because of our sluggish destiny. Deprived, we just can't attain the dust of the Lord's feet. ShriLalit Kishore Devji displayed the celestial nature of Vrindavan as perceived from Golok; the lyrical flow of the Yamuna, clouds showering rain like flowers, peacocks dancing in ecstasy, birds singing passionately, blooming blossoms and creepers embracing tree trunks, bees dancing around lotus pollen, flying birds and cranes, cows drawn towards the flute and six glorious seasons.

Vrinda is one of the foremost sixteen names of Shri Radha, as revealed by the Holy Scriptures. Initially, Lord Krishna had created Vrindavan in Golok for Shri Radha and the earthly Vrindavan made for her pleasure and amorous frolic is just a mirrored illusion, a temporal reflection of the eternal Vrindavan, where God dwells forever. Here, life exists because of Lord Krishna's devotion. People captivated by mysteries and mazes of the Lord's leelas, animals and birds entranced by his melodious flute play stand-still as if nature is enchanted by some passionate frenzy.

There are several green forests within Vrindavan, holy mountains awash with creepers and green pastures beneficial for cattle, not merely providing comfort to the cows, gopas and gopikas but deserving their servitude. One sakhi tells another that this Vrindavan propagates its fame right up to Vaikuntha because it is marked by the lotus feet of Shri Krishna. When he plays his mellifluous flute, peacocks dance in ecstasy and animals and birds hovering over the mountain peaks are calmed. The flowers and creepers blossom for serving Shri Radha, who nurtures them herself. Every site of Vrindavan is most fortunate because Shri Radha has trod upon it. The passionate singing of birds in the nikunjas enhances the beauty of the place, making everyone exquisitely desirous to wander in this celestial land. Shri Radha and Krishna are grateful to Vrindavan, where their love sport unfolds, interspersed with the pathos of longing and the joy of belonging.

Vrindavaneshwari

tapta-kanchana-gaurangi
radhevrndavanesvari
vrsabhanu-sutedevi
pranamamihari-priye

- SrilaPrabhupada

It is next to impossible to think about Krishna, Vrindavan, the trees and nature without our beloved Kishoriji. Shriradha rani resides in the heart of Vrindavan alongside Krishna. Throughout the world, Krishna is praised and worshipped. But it is only after years of ardently loving the mysterious divine god that one understands Radha. It is not Krishna that devotees fall in love with, rather it is Radha Rani, the queen of hearts that controls our Madhava, and hence, controls us as well. Radha is the most baffling amongst all the female deities in the Hindu pantheon. She is the supreme goddess, a divine feminine energy. The mahamantra is a prayer to Shri Radha rani, to engage us in lord Krishna's service. From Radha, all the other female energies have

been born. She is the source of shakti, she is the cosmic energy. Krishna tells Radha, "Know that prakriti and purusha are the same. We have two bodies but the soul is identical."

Radha rani is not only the consort of Shri Krishna; she is the goddess of love and devotion. Devotion for Radha rani is the easiest way to surrender to Krishna as Radha- Krishna are one, they are the same. To differentiate between them does no good to anybody. For a millennial like me, it was hard to let go of all my preconceived notions about various gods and goddesses and the toughest part was to stop looking at gods from a religious point of view. We live in a country where we have always witnessed the divisions made among the gods by us, where we have always seen each other imposing our thoughts and conditions on Him, The Supreme Godhead. But every time, we fail to understand that everything cannot be divided among religions and boundaries, especially love and devotion. Spiritual connection with Radha-Krishna has nothing to do with what culture; sect or gender a person is from. They see us alike; therefore, we are absolutely nobody to put a stop at something which has not ever been in our control, to divide devotion in religions, in different forms.

Devotion is a connection of the soul with the lord, bhava, prem, and it is purely spiritual. It is what your antarmann (soul) longs for. Societal restrictions are for those who do harm. It is not to be feared by those who have surrendered to him. By breaking free of societal norms and restrictions, Radharani loved Krishna, her love for Krishna was parishudh (pure) as she did not fear the society. She did not fear what others might say, what others might think and this is why she became one with Shri Krishna. She was always engrossed in the thoughts of Shri Krishna and she showered him with utmost love. We do not really find any word of Kishoriji in the ShrimadBhagavatam or in the Mahabharata. These are the two highly reputed holy books if one has to read about Krishna. It is so strange that his beloved is not mentioned in any of these, isn't it? Well, it is solely because Radharani is the bhava (feeling) of Krishna. She is Krishna and she is a part of Krishna, so when we talk about Kishore, Kishoriji is automatically joined with him. There are only a few books that Radha rani has been mentioned in, one of the books which mention her is the BrahmavaivartaPurana. BrahmavaivartaPurana was composed in the later stage, this book talks about Radha as the highest consort of Krishna, his consort even in the splendid, celestial Goloka. According to this book, Radha rani was cursed by Shridama, a devotee of Shri Krishna to be born in the mortal world. We cannot savor the romantic sentiment without the beloved as love requires not only the self but it equally requires the object of love for its expression, which here is KishoriRadha. Radha is acknowledged with the supreme deity for she controls Krishna with her love, and perfect spiritual life is unattainable without her grace. In the sensuous lyrics of Gita Govinda by Jayadeva, Shri Radha rani is exalted as

Shrikrishna's hladinishakti or blissful energy. In a way, after understanding the Swaroopa of Radha, I started to understand Krishna. Radha's name is always said before taking Krishna's name, as Radha is dearest to him. For a devotee, the highest achievement is to please Radha as pleasing her gives us an insight into true devotion, prem. In some places, she is the principal idol of devotion and the symbol of divine love. There is no greater symbol to denote the longing of the soul in its quest for the divine than the characterization of Radharani. To this day, many people who visit the Radhakunda sit in the holy place where Radharani had set foot in.

PremRasamritDhara: Letter No 17

Shri Dham Vrindavan

Priya Vijay,

"Krsnematirastu" [Let your attention be on Krsna's feet"]

Ever since I came back after meeting you at ShriVrishbhanupur, I have been thinking of writing a letter to you but somehow it got delayed.

Spontaneously liberating you from worldly bonds, the infinite mercy of Krishna has bestowed residence at Shri RadhaKund. What greater act of compassion can there be?

All that you have to do is to properly utilise dark-hued Krishna's loving tenderness bestowed on you and that too, thoughtfully and conscientiously. This is the only task you have to do. The Supreme Lover's grace and hand that grants blessings always accompany a virtuous act.

Residence at a spiritual site and detachment are the means and not the destination. This is a fact to be remembered at all times. Not forgetting the truth that 'gantavyasthal', the destination site, is our supreme and ultimate goal and the object of human pursuit. An ardent longing is essential for reaching our destination, which can in turn help us reach our spiritual goal.

Krishna, the Supreme Object of worship, is dependent on svarupa and our relationship with Him. No matter how tough a sadhana we have done, no matter how intensely detached we are, if we are not passionately serious and long for connection with the svarupa of Krishna, there is no possibility of attaining the Supreme Object.

Narada Bhakti Sutra

Narad Bhakti Sutra:' tad vismaraneparamvyakulta' only in this state of intense longing is it possible to spontaneously forget about the mundane world. Only when one forgets about his/her own loved ones, family members, and gurus is the feeling of closeness to the Supreme Object possible. Otherwise, hard work and effort is all that remains. Consequently, we get a minimum amount of profit or return.

Solely focusing our thoughts upon Krishna and remembering Him and letting His lila or divine play hover over and pervade every fiber of our being is what is required. Our thoughts are to be overpowered by His beauteous form, gunas, and loving tenderness. Furthermore, we must even forget who we are and who our well-wishers are. Alongside a concentrated internal practice of imaginative recollection by living through the countless playful legends of Radha and

Krishna is a must.

Only then is it possible to slightly relish His beauteous form and ineffable beauty. If we do not adopt this course, there is danger of extreme delay.

Our mind has to be constantly absorbed in meditating upon Lord Krishna's lila or divine play. Striving towards not letting other thoughts weigh on our mind is what is most essential. Considering virtuous deeds to be nurturing, our remembrance of Krishna is also a hurdle in our path. If we want to attain Supreme Object Krishna as soon as possible, we should forever be possessed and overwhelmed by His form and gunas.

You must have probably understood what I am trying to say. Everything is fine here. Pay my regards to Shri RadhaKund which is the svarupa of Shri Radha.

Jai Radhe,
Yours Manohar Das

This letter describes the holiness of Radha rani, and that even water touched by her is worth worshiping. Whilst writing this, I was so deeply in the prem(love) for Radha rani and Krishna that I totally forgot about telling you how I reached this point. Well, every human is very egocentric; at certain stages, we surely do selfless deeds that make us happy for a moment. But other than that we generally look at the bhavana (feeling) of 'I'. it might be easy to let go of this while someone starts devotional practices but keeping this in control is very hard. It is what a lot of people call 'impossible' as us humans are sowed and reaped with desires, ambitions, and lust, all humanly. Well, these aren't so humanly if you think about it. All these desires are for us, none benefit the society and even if slight chances any of these benefit the greater goal, we really do not do that because of that certain reason. It is generally for our own benefit. The first thing I did was humble myself down. I was never a snooty prick, but I always had utmost pride in myself, which sometimes went in the very wrong and negative direction. Keeping my ego in check helped me improve my wordly relationships as well. One of the very fine examples of selflessness would be the Asthasakhis, also known as the eight principal friends of ShrimatiRadharani. These asthsakhis are Lalitadevi, Vishakha Devi, Champakalata Devi, Chitra Devi, Tungavidya Devi, Indulekha Devi, Rangadevidevi and Sudevi. Why are these gopis the primary, the principal sakhis? Well, because their motives were solely for the divine couple and all their practices were solely to get Radha Krishna together. They loved both of them alike. Their delight was to see the divine couple together. Each sakhi (friend) had a different quality but the same goal. Among these eight sakhis, the prime ashtasakhi is Lalitadevi. She is hot-tempered was also the leader of these sakhis. She used to arrange the rendezvous of Radha and Krishna. SrilaRupa Goswami prays,"I offer pranama again and again unto Srimati Lalitadevi."

Sri Vishaka is the second most important of the ashtasakhis. Vishakhaji is known to be very intelligent and expert at giving advice to the divine couple. Vishakhadevi is also known as the river Yamuna. This reminds the divine couple of each other every moment. Lalitadevi and Vishakhadevi are prime examples of sakhis who are svapaksa to Radha rani. Their affection towards Radha rani stands supreme. The third sakhi is Champakalata, she is known to be an expert at the art of logical persuasion, a diplomat. Chitradevi, the fourth sakhi can easily find out the intention behind any activity. She is very learned as well. The fifth sakhi, Tunga vidya can communicate with birds and animals.

She is considered to be very hot-tempered but also very learned as she possesses the gyan, knowledge of the vedas. Sakhi Indulekha is very knowledgeable in sciences and in topics about snakes. She also possesses knowledge about palmistry and gemology.

Rangadevi is witty yet diplomatic. She is an expert at logic as she attained various boons. The last ashtasakhi, Sudevi, is known to look like Radha rani's sister. She is always alongside Radha to deck her up at all times. All these sakhis together made sure that the love between Radha and Krishna never extinguishes; even after their separation on the earth, these sakhis did not for once lose their prembhava for the divine couple. We humans are so full of emotions. Sometimes, due to various mood swings, it gets hard for us to understand our own emotions. In this state, helping others is a long lost thought as we cannot even figure out what we need at that particular moment. Born in the mortal world, the ashtasakhis kept the needs, desires and the feelings of the divine couple their top most priority. This is what bhakti is. This is the kind of love that Shree and Shreeji teach us. In this weary world it is very important to get our emotions in our control and it is very important to keep Krishna in our thoughts. I achieved this by chanting the holy name, the name of the creator, the godhead Shri Krishna. A sense of calmness took over my soul in every word that came out of my mouth as it was about him and his consort, Radha rani.

It is rather hard to understand Radha rani and her relationship with Krishna if we go snooping around in books, as the feeling of love as theirs cannot be written down in a few pages. Moreover, it cannot be understood by those who do not surrender unto the feet of the goddess. We all have bhava (emotions) but Radha rani is mahabhava.

In the Adilila Chapter 4 verse 69 it is given:

SriRadhaThakurani is the embodiment of mahabhava. She is the repository of all good qualities and the crest jewel among all the lovely consorts of Lord Krishna.

Purport

The unadulterated action of the hladinisakti is displayed in the dealings of the damsels of Vraja and SrimatiRadharani, who is the topmost participant in that transcendental group. The essence of hladinisakti is the love of Godhead, the essence of the love of Godhead is bhava, or transcendental sentiment, and the highest pitch of that bhava is called mahabhava. SrimatiRadharani is the personified embodiment of all aspects of transcendental consciousness. She is therefore the highest principle in love of Godhead and is the supreme lovable object of SriKrishna.

FIVE

Anant

In the very beginning I had mentioned that my grandfather is the one who has these long, everlasting debates with me after such matters. It is always better to have a conversation with someone who is willing to show you the other side as well. Every day, he used to test my knowledge in order to get the idea of whether I actually understand anything. He never shot any direct questions at me. It always used to be like him throwing slightly crooked statements and I jumping in right there to correct it and finally, one day, I noticed how he smiled after I corrected him about one of the few mistakes he had made. That day, I understood that even though he has so much more knowledge than I possess, he acted like he did not know a lot, just for me, so that I learn more and move forward on the path to reach Krishna. This changed my attitude towards knowledge and it is not just what we learn from our education system, it comes from the brahmand (the universe), it is divine, and it is a way to live. Knowledge shapes a person, even if a person is very knowledgeable or has the highest IQ, if that person does not bow down to Krishna, that knowledge is useless, and that knowledge will just get the person through this mortal world. How we choose to act and what we choose to do with our knowledge really define us as a person. It is not for everybody to let go of material beliefs and be lost in Ghanshyama. According to the Bhagavad Gita, verse 15.5-

nirmāna-mohājita-saṅga-doṣā
adhyātma-nityāvinivṛtta-kāmāḥ
dvandvairvimuktāḥsukha-duḥkha-saṁjñair
gacchantyamūḍhāḥpadamavyayaṁ tat

Which means that the one who is free from illusion, false prestige, and false association, who understands the eternal, who is done with material lust and is freed from the duality of happiness and distress, and who knows how to surrender unto the supreme personality attains the eternal kingdom? There is nothing in this universe that has a higher position than the spiritual master, Krishna. From the beginning, I have heard his name as I had already mentioned and that sure does help in pushing one over to this direction but spirituality is attainable only when one decides to follow the path. Nitya Kishori, Radha rani, the way she loved Krishna is not from this world, it is celestial yet this whole lila (play) took place on this planet. Now it is obviously up to others to believe in this or not but if one puts even a pinch of an effort to understand the lilas of ManmohanaShri Krishna, it does not take long to fall deeply in love with him.

A person's intention, their behavior is a very important part of bhakti. Now one may ask 'why?' A person who is a true devotee of Krishna has a pure and huge heart; they have unending compassion for all living beings, all the nature present on this earth. If a person chanting Krishna's name is rude, mean, egoistic, and lacks compassion, then such a person can never be a true devotee, because a true devotee sees parts and parcels of Krishna in everybody. Therefore, they treat everybody with utmost love and compassion. We live in a world where people are quick to judge the mythological stories presented to us. They distinguish any beliefs of the Supreme Personality's existence on this Earth, and such people have never truly tried to connect with him. 'What is the proof of Krishna's existence?' someone asked me initially when I started reading the Gita. At that moment, as I had no answer, I told that person politely, "I do not know the answer to that right now, but once I do, I will surely get back to you." Time passed by and I remembered this particular conversation and I decided to call that person. We had a conversation about various things and suddenly, I brought up the question that was asked months ago. To my surprise, my friend started laughing and questioned if I had really found the answer.

My answer shortly followed, "Krishna is divy(divine), Krishna is paramatma (supreme soul), Krishna is achook (infallible), he is ajam(unborn), pavitram(purest), shashwatam(eternal), adidivam(originator), vibhum (greatest) and dharm(sacred)."

To describe Krishna is not difficult but it surely is difficult to understand him. Those who do not believe in him and those who do not surrender to him can never know him. He is the divine knowledge and he is the utmost joy. Everything originates from him and everything ends at him as well. Everything in between is just a web of life. In the Bhagavat Gita verse 7.25

nāhaṁprakāśaḥsarvasya

yoga-māyā-samāvṛtaḥ

mūḍho 'yaṁnābhijānāti

lokomāmajamavyayam

This means that, I (Krishna) never manifest to the foolish and unintelligent. For them I am covered by my eternal creative potency [yoga-māyā]; and so the deluded world knows me not, who am unborn and infallible.

Therefore, to understand Krishna, one has to attain the path of him, and wherever Krishna is, Radha rani is also present .When the divine couple took birth on this planet, they taught us love, bhakti, and knowledge, which is remembered by so many. Every person walking in the streets of the VrindavanDham always has Radha rani's name on their lips. Lucky are those who get to be around the heart of the leelas RadhaKrishna did on earth. Even when beloved Krishna was born, during his naming ceremony, the saint had already astonished everybody when he uttered that this boy will do many wonders. Shri

Gargacharyaji was highly learned and the family priest of NandRaiji. "The dark-hued boy is incarnated in every era. Because of his complexion, the colour of the condensed sky, he will be called Krishna. Born to Vasudev, he will be addressed as Vasudev by those who knew this secret. The lad would be a trove of several names and virtues. He is virtually the same as Lord Narayana regarding glory, power, qualities, and wealth. Dearly loved by all Braj denizens, Lord Krishna will be their saviour, expiating all sins and alleviating pain." exclaimed the muni. Such is the divinity of Krishna. He is highly revered by Vaishnavas till date.

The philosophy
of emotions

"Feed your faith and all your doubts shall starve to death."
– Gaur Gopal Das

Mahabhava is the greatest feeling. Bhava is a feeling as well as an emotion. We all have emotions, right? Some people express it well, while others shy away from opening up in front of an audience of people, but we all do have oceans of different emotions flowing right through us. Some make us happy whereas the rest feel like a burden on our soul. Emotions vary from person to person and from situation to situation. They are subjective in nature, yet we all have such definitive diction, and set means to these words. It is very funny and at the same time very upsetting that most of us refrain from expressing ourselves, maybe because of the limitations we have. Throughout my early childhood I tried to stay within the set norms of when, where, and

how I am supposed to express my emotions. It did not matter if I was breaking up inside. If it is not considered an appropriate reaction by the society, I am to conceal it, no matter what. Since the very beginning, I have had a very zealous life. Even though I tried putting away my questions for the major part of it, I still asked because every answer I got made me a little happier. Whether we accept it or not, we humans are very xenophobic. We tend to fit in because it is just so scary to step out of that zone, to explore. What if we might not like what we see? And it all boils down to "if I leave, will I find someone to share my emotions with?" We all bear the flag of truth and honesty on our shoulders but the harsh truth is that none of us are veracious; none of us are even truthful to ourselves, let alone the world. Throughout our lives, we tend to live along the lines of the society and try to fit in even though that is not the purpose of our lives. We are to break free; now, the people who want to take this in the negative context will do so no matter what I say, right? But breaking free is choosing what to express, when to express, and how to express. We should not be subjugated to the society. We all have been granted a free will to follow a path that is to be created by us, a path that not only gives us immense satisfaction and happiness but also provides us enlightenment to connect with the divine, especially our Y-generation, that tends to overlook the joy, the beauty of life, the calm in the divine, and the liberation in love. We all have such a pathetic theory of what life is all about. Wealth not only measures substantial happiness for us, but it also is a sign as to how mannered a person is. The basic personality, characteristics, and knowledge play a very small part in today's world. So, even though Krishna said that just his name is enough to reach him, in kalayug, we tend to not even be able to do that with full concentration, with utmost devotion. This era specifically lacks basic equanimity. Yes, education plays a major role in shaping one's future but more than that, our confidence in ourselves, compassion towards others, and having faith in god is what really carves the road towards our future. It does not mold us into a person, it solidifies us to flow through every situation life has to offer with a smile on our face.

Initially, in my high school days, I used to have a great deal of temper, such that even a small situation used to make me sad to such a point I could ruin the whole party. With time and with learning at each step, I started to understand that whatever happens, HAPPENS FOR A REASON. Everybody blurts out this line every now and then, I have also heard it ample number of times, but it is what it is, the truth of life. Nothing happens without any purpose attached to it. You lost a friend whom you had considered to be friends with for the rest of your lives because they didn't look at you in the same capacity. Life does throw very difficult situations at us at every point of time. It is not easy to accept the reality of life but once we start to live with it and accept it with open arms, it becomes a tad bit easier.

Nobody can reverse or change what is written for us but all of us can surrender to Krishna, as he is someone who never leaves our side. He never does let go. He would not change the working of life for us; he gives us immense strength to accept our fate. At the end of the day, he is always there, holding our hand and walking us through to his loka (his abode) when this is all over. People suffer from major megalomania; they always forget the power of humility and the importance of being humble. However important we may find ourselves, we need to understand that we are small living entities who survive in a huge universe, which is a small, tiny part of the creation of godhead. We can never be big enough to not thank him for everything that he has provided us with. Sharing with others is the basic quality of life, so if one forgets his/her roots, then even though they may achieve great heights, they might not receive pleasure or a sense of satisfaction in that work.

When I started with this journey, I was on a quest to find myself, but I found Krishna instead. I have discovered a lot. We humans have various otherworldly relationships that give us immense strength to keep going. What we perceive or how we see things plays such an important role in the growth of relationships. When I started writing, it was about who I was and what my experience has been like... yet throughout this journey, a couple of my friends have supported and equally helped me to work towards that goal. Such friendships are very hard to come across these days. When I noticed how people around me bring about certain changes in me, it was very important for me to understand what people generally think about love.

SEVEN

Contemporary relish

"It is strange that sword and words have the same letters. Even more strange is that they have the same effect if not handled properly."

— Gaur Gopal Das

Love is an emotion that is present in all relations as it is the primary stone to the foundation for anything to blossom upon. I asked just two questions from a certain number of people, these two questions bring about the basic reality in front of us. The first question was 'according to you, what is love?' Such an easy question, isn't it? When I popped up this question, I assumed well what is in the their hearts will get down on the paper, but instead, I got replies to a different question, which was 'according to you, what is ideal love?' Everyone answered what they thought was the most ideal form of love, whereas nobody really understood the whole emotion behind the short word. We carry this notion that love is a feeling between two people, who, in today's words, are 'dating each other' whereas this feeling is

behind every single emotion that we see around ourselves. We love our close friends and we love our parents. Therefore, to simply bind this one with just that one relationship takes away the whole meaning behind it.

One of the answers that I received was - "So, what it actually is for me is that it is supposed to be selfless. Like in the downs and in the ups too. The kind in which the partners support each other rather than being toxic, you know? Just like hypothetically, if I am getting an opportunity to go to a place which will enhance my skills and that place is far away, my partner should support me and persuade me to go for it rather that holding me back. If it is toxic even at the slightest level, it is not love."

Well, to the naked eye, there is absolutely nothing wrong with this answer, but if we dive deeper to the emotional level, this calls for expectations. If we are expecting support in return of our support then it is not selfless. It is just love with conditions, the conditions being that you have to do as I do or else this would not work out. But what if I love someone truly from the bottom of my heart? It should not matter whether he is my partner or not, the only thing that should matter is that I love and respect that particular person to always wish the best for him.

Out of the many people I asked to answer this question, only one person stood out, and the answer I received went like this, "For me, loving someone is nothing but healing yourself. You grow immensely within and even on the outside when you are in love. Loving can never come without caring either, one of the very important things for me is taking care of the person whom you love; in fact, you tend to like things which your lover likes or does. Love is the power by which one could heal the world by solving problems of just one person, the one you love. It makes you feel how beautiful the world is, even with all the chaos. One should always take care and tell their loved ones how much you love them and mean for them."

So this might seem just similar to the previous answer, yet in many ways, it is not. Yes, this answer also implies that the feeling of love is felt towards a lover, but not necessarily, it grows deeper than that. It is about caring, it is about respecting. This does not talk about wanting love in return for love; it simply puts out the feeling of unconditional love for all the important people in one's life.

Through this answer, I basically understood how people understand that there is a feeling, an emotion that is love. They assume it is beautiful but most people tend to forget the essence of this as they still have walls of conditions up ahead of them. The second question which I asked from the same group of people was –"what do you think love for today's generation is like?" and this was a pretty funny one. The reason for that is solely that the same people who believe in a concept called love have an idea of what this feeling is supposed to be like, and somewhere, they believe they are in the realm of giving that sort of love to people around them. These same people highly feel that the world around them does not understand this word at all. So either it is with how people express does not get through to the other person because if everyone carries a similar idea of love why is it people feel love is basically lost in the world? With huge paragraphs received by me as the first answer the second answer was fairly a one line game. Some of the similar replies I received for this question basically summed it up in this one line - "They often confuse love with lust, and that makes love lose its essence" and "god knows"

Funny enough, isn't it? Well, it is how scared we are to put our heart on the platter, it is about how wrongly we perceive the other person's intention and the worst of all is naming things relationship which are highly toxic for us in this world. We always tend to run behind that which is not meant to be healthy for us as we seek great thrill in chasing someone. We are a very crooked generation with various expectations and opposite behaviors. For some, love is delusional while for others, it is a long lost concept but what surprises me the most is that love for others in our generation is hurtful. It is toxic and polluted. One person walked up to me as I was about to close this topic and focus on the next one and gave me a reply that did hurt my soul as well. I could clearly make out that the person has been deeply hurt as I could listen to the voice of the person trembling as she spoke to me about love.

"It's just a way of hurting yourself since you never learn

to actually do as you say. It is like the fresh morning breeze but it keeps getting polluted with time passing and at the end, it is so toxic that it becomes hard to breathe, but you still try to stand the weather. After a while, everybody eventually gives up. You finally walk past it and you get a new morning, but this new morning does not last forever, does it? You meet another person, it all seems lovely and yet again you find yourself caught up in the same cycle and it eventually ends up in people walking out the door. It really does hurt."

To even hear something like this got me wondering as to how emotionally drained most of us have become, how pathetic a life we all have been living where we end up hurting the people we supposedly love. It is a strange world to live in. With getting pristine degrees, we assume ourselves to be the masters of knowledge. It does not matter what the topic is, we think we know it all. It is not at all difficult these days, with just one click on the net, we can get answers to every single question. It does not matter how accurate it is, but since it is accessible by all, we assume it to be true.

EIGHT

The essence of love

Love is not love until you actually get so invested that you're just consumed by love.

Now, I did touch upon the topic of is the meaning of love. There is not really any negative side to this word. It encompasses all the positivity in the world one can only imagine. One website accessed by each and every person reading this book at the moment, is Wikipedia. Well, we all have used Wikipedia to do our research projects for school or college. I somehow happened to ask Wikipedia 'What is love?', and the answer I got was totally opposite of what I am trying to explain here. The definition according to the website goes on to say - "Love is considered to be a positive and negative: with its virtue representing human kindness, compassion, and affection, as "the unselfish loyal and benevolent concern for the good of another"; and its vice representing human moral flaw akin to vanity, selfishness, amour-porpe and egotism, as it potentially leads people into a type of mania, obsessiveness, or codependency. It

may also describe compassionate and affectionate actions towards other humans, one's self or animals. In its various forms, love acts as a major facilitator of interpersonal relationships and, owing to its central psychological importance, is one of the most common themes in the creative arts. Love has been postulated to be a function to keep human beings together against menaces and to facilitate the continuation of the species."

Now if we understand love according to the above given definition, we are surely doomed. Giving negatives to something so pure basically extinguishes the whole feeling, the bhava of the emotion. The line 'facilitate the continuation of the species' has absolutely nothing to do with love. Well, two human beings wanting to procreate for whatever reason is the sole reason for procreation. If one person does not love his/her partner but they have to procreate due to familial pressure, then we cannot call that love just because they are continuing their species. Just because they have given birth to their offspring, this is totally out of context. Now this particular line that says "Biological models of sex tend to view love as a mammalian drive, much like hunger or thirst" really did put me off. It is very common today to perceive love as lust. The ardent sexual desire is often confused as love by this generation but these two are not similar in any way.

Now what love looks like is what the Shyam-Shyama teach us, commonly known as Radha Krishna to our generation.

Shyam mei hai Radheya Radhe mei hai Shyam, lag eek dehdujas was ho abhivahn.

A love not understood by any of us mortal, materialistic human beings, the love of Radha Krishna. Unlike what most of us have heard in fables, Radha and Krishna are never separated, they are always present with each other if not in physical form then in an emotional bond, which most of us do not understand. Radharani, as radiant as a thousand suns and as luminous as a full moon took birth on this loka(planet) to teach all of us about love and bhakti. The story of RadhaKrishna did not originate on this planet, nor did it end here. This story began in the celestial sky, even when the solar system was not created, in the holy abode of Goloka, RadhaKrishna's eternal place.

A conflict between affection and anxiety arises within our minds when we think about love, doesn't it? The estranged feeling of losing the other person, the conflict between love and selfishness. These feelings, however different they might sound, have perplexed each and every human being at one point or another. The idea of love that we carry (especially our generation) is so much based on the conditions and questions and fears, and these things combined never give us the answers to the very simple question 'what is love, is it really there?' The very simple explanation to love is that there is no explanation to this term, as it is a feeling as pure as the holy waters of the Ganges and as pious as Radha's feelings for Krishna. Love and affection are the basis of any known relationship, be it companionship, parent-child relationship or any other relation, named or unnamed. Yet in this bewildered world, caught within the materialistic fortunes and unending pity, we make these our desire. When this desire arises, two human beings no longer remain equal, because then we get the feeling of 'I', 'mein', 'me' and as soon as this feeling creeps in, we lose the concept of love. It is because of these ardent desires that we tend to control the other person's emotions. Love is not about selfishness, it is the most holy feeling in the world which should not be polluted by the premonitions of what today's relationships look like. It is to surrender oneself, it is to liberate, and it is to respect. This is the kind of love that Radha-Krishna teache us. It is love that is present in the heart at all times even if one is detached from the other person. It is faith in oneself and faith in the other person, this feeling is love. Proving one's love is the stupidest thing that is done, as something as pure as Godhead Shri Krishna himself need not be proved. Love is not just a four-letter word, it is a feeling not realized by many. It is surrendering without losing yourself. It is free from krodh (anger), aham (self-importance), ahankar (ego), and moh (attraction). It is all sufficient. It is the feeling of giving, abundance of love. With various conditions placed upon us, by us and by the society, we start believing that love is nothing but a liking towards another person whereas this feeling is of unconditional love, the feeling of everflowing devotion towards Krishna. This feeling that we all strive to achieve can solely be understood by loving Radha-Krishna, and then in this mortal world, we overcome our desires to surrender ourselves to utmost love.

Well, I knew that what I see on the surface is just a façade and that I will eventually have to dig deeper to find answers to the questions I was looking for. After a while, everyone who goes on a quest to find enlightenment realizes that it is more important to bring about the necessary changes in one's lifestyle so as to attain the mercy of the divine couple than reaching a certain point of knowing the truth. So, a lot of people have this question in their minds as to why Krishna is the epitome of love.

As Radha rani is mahabhava, Krishna is parishudhprem (pure love). Radha-Krishna are also known by the names of each other, such is their love. Radha rani is also known as Krishna Priya, which means the beloved of Shri Krishna and Krishna is also known as Radhavallabha, lover of ShrimatiRadha rani. Just like their names, they co-exist. Their romantic dalliances are extremely pristine and totally stripped of lust.

PremRasamritDhara: Letter No 20

Priya Vijay,

VrindavanDham

"Krsnematirastu"[Let your attention be on Krsna's feet"] Received your letter.

The path of love is so strange. Prema or pure love does not expect love in Return. There is no doubt that one does get love in return. However, the lover does not keep this fact in mind and loves just because he has to. In addition, he has to bear the anguish of separation. If someone nurses him it is fine but if someone doesn't, then also it is fine. He just has to love.

Do prema is not an appropriate word. It is the

instinctive trait of prema but this is the middling state. The Supreme Lover is ultimately mesmerized by the beloved. It is His very nature to be controlled by prema. Action or thought have no accessibility to this state. There is no place for disappointment if there is everlasting hope.

Watered by prema, the creeper of hope grows. Clinging to every limb of the Supreme Lover, the creeper gets entwined in each fiber of our being. It is the creeper's nature to cling and it is the Supreme Lover Krishna's nature to become entwined. This divine play, an interaction between the Supreme Lover and the beloved, takes place daily.

A true, selfless, and loving resolve is of utmost important. Promptness or delay depends on the intensity of our ardent longing. Pure thoughts, devoid

of other intrusive and disturbing ones, quickly bring the desired Supreme Object Krishna close to us. The cluster of samskaras or innate impressions is washed away by our yearning and gush of love for Krishna.

In this manner, samskaras or inborn impressions are naturally turned to ashes in a mind passionately drawn to dark-hued Krishna. But all this depends on the intensity of our longing. True longing never goes waste. Yearning is a source of attraction. Attraction and a passionate craving for Krishna are no different.

We can call it an ardent longing or being a worthy recipient. Attaining the Supreme Object Krishna depends on how passionate one is as a recipient. Supreme Object Krishna is laden with rasa and fickle. How strongly Krishna is drawn to a recipient depends on the shape of the receiver. It is the very nature of the Supreme Lover to take on the shape of the receiving container. Connection with Krishna is the unique trait of being a worthy recipient. Attachment resides in striking a close relationship with Krishna. There is music, merriment, and a connection with Krishna when we love Him.

With Love,

Yours Bobo

This letter beautifully describes what prema (love) is, or at least gets our attention on what prem (love) is supposed to look like. Krishna is full of prem, it is just a matter of time when one realizes how easy and calming it is to surrender to the lotus feet of the supreme, and once that is done, we find new meaning in all the worldly relations as well, and we find bhava from within ourselves. I was probably in grade 6th when I first told my father about a very good looking boy whom I liked, basically he was my best friend and being so young, I assumed it to be a completely different emotion. The next thing I know my father was smiling and laughing out loud to my statement, which left me in a very weird position as I could barely understand the reaction that I had just received. Well, after so many years, I probably do. I have always had a knack for understanding things very quickly; I just need to put my heart and soul in it. It really depends on how much of this we see as a sacrifice and how much we see as a road to godhead. If we start seeing this from a point of view of sacrifice, then in a sense it would mean that we are giving up on something that was dear to us whereas in this, nothing and nobody is dearer to us than the divine couple.

NINE

The prestigious bonding

Feeling the oneness of yourself with all things is true love

- Eckhart Tolle

Leelas? What are Leelas? When we talk about Krishna we talk about his leelas, which can be translated to 'his divine plays.' Everything about Krishna, starting from his janma (birth) to incidents leading to the war of Mahabharata, everything is divine. We cannot put our finger on any particular thing from his life and put him in the same category as other humans.

He was born in a prison in the city of Mathura, displaying divine energy, spreading joy as well as delight. It is believed that when Krishna was born, conch shells starting blowing and all the flowers starting blossoming. Lord Krishna was then taken to Gokul, to his foster parents Nand and Yashoda. At a very tender age, Krishna showed Yashoda maa the whole brahmand (universe) in his tiny mouth. His divine plays kept following shortly. His maternal uncle, Kans attacked him various number of times, sending demonic energies to finish little Krishna off, but he killed all of these demons in a fraction of a second.

Romantic dalliances of Lord Krishna, Divine Incarnate, constantly prevail in the nikunjas, banks of the Yamuna and at wells. In the new millennium, this ethereal land rejoices with tinkling anklets and resounds with the dark God fluting in its blossoming pastures. It is our vision which is blurred and ears deafened with worldly clatter...because of which we are unable to conceptualize his divine play. Several dedicated devotees have seen these dalliances and are doing so. Krishna used to spend a lot of time playing on the slopes of Mount Giriraj, also known as Govardhanparvat to all of us. At a very tender age, Krishna admonished the people of the Vrajnot for falling prey to ritualistic Vedic worship rather than practicing humanistic dharma, love. He asked the people to worship Govardhanparvat, as this mountain provided pasture lands for the cattle as well as a playground for the children. Seeing this, when Indra showered heavy rains continuously, Krishna lifted the whole mountain on his tiny finger, protecting everyone from the gut wrenching rains. The Bhagavata posits Lord Krishna as the paragon of sweetness and gives him epithets such as madhukarya or madhupati. Krishna's life is known to be filled with dangers as well as uncountable delights. Having killed so many demons and defeating Devraj Indra, Krishna delighted everyone in Braj with playful pranks. Krishna spent his early childhood as a cowherd among the simple people of Braj. These are the leelas that happened in the early childhood of Krishna. After this, he travelled to Mathura as a young man. Krishna killed his evil uncle and freed his parents, Devaki and

Vasudev. During this period, he established a kingdom known as Dwaraka, which was surrounded by luxury, and there was a palace made of gold. How can Krishna, who rid this earth of evil, be considered a human? He took birth on this planet for various reasons and this was one of them.

When talking about Krishna leela, the divine play, the leelas that are at the paramount are the rasa leelas. People really confuse these rasa leelas with something that is so full of lust and sexual desires and really dumb down the cosmic energies, the divine love, and the sheer happiness that these provide the devotees. I still remember when I was very young, my parents used to take me to Vrindavandham and at night, there used to be Rasa leela enactments. I do not remember much of that, but yes, once I grew up to an age where I started to comprehend more clearly, some devotees called the rasa mandali to our city to perform and by the end of it, everybody was overjoyed. We cannot see these stories happening. All we can do is to keep them in our memories, a mere human enactment of the divine play managed to get everybody teary, so one can only imagine how beautiful the rasa with Krishna would be. The love of the gopis is seen as a transcendental love of the highest order, so why would his hungering devotees think of anything else? Mere thoughts of rasa are nothing but elation and ecstasy.

Rasa has no beginning, no end, no order, no sequence, and no comparison. There are no words to express it, no ears to listen to it and no mind in which it can be contained. If rasa itself has managed to create a place to reside in, then there is the mind, eyes, ears and every fiber of one's being to taste it. But if rasa becomes the vantage point of rasa then there are no eyes, ears, nose, and tongue to relish it. Eyes are seeing, ears are listening, and the tongue is talking about the supreme form in which the Primordial self is contained. The mind, eyes, ears, tongue, body, and every fiber of our being are rasa. Rasa created this charming nature for relishing its own joy. Both, Shri Radha, the Beloved and Krishna, the Supreme Lover, are an integral part of rasa, as they dally and play with each other.

'*Tum nikat main nikat tam*', this bhava of nearness has indeed arisen from Shri Radha Krishna. Both are near each other and this leads to a romantic dalliance taking place at that very moment. ShriRadha-Krishna, heading for mutual union. The miracle of the Rasa Leela, that supreme moment of Krishna's manifestation as a human lover and divine incarnate dancing with the gopis in the forest of Vrindavan and bathing with them in the flowing water of the Yamuna on the radiant night of SharadPoornima, is a moment of purity and effulgence visited over and over again through centuries. Lord Krishna, the supreme lover with his beloved ShriRadha and gopis on the celestial banks of the Yamuna, in the dense nikunjas, in the light of the full moon, commenced the rapturous dance, holding hands to complete a circle. Amidst the idyllic environs and showering merriment, the tempo grew faster and faster. Krishna duplicated himself through his maya so that between two gopis was found a Krishna, sporting with them in the magical dance of the Raas Mandala. He assumed as many forms as was necessary to make each one happy. The gopi bhava is love and pristine kam, the zenith of spiritual awareness. The undivided whole that is God requires the absorption of its parts to be restored to wholeness once again.

Gopivallabha or beloved of the gopis is one of Lord Krishna's epithets. Udhavaji says that the hearts of the gopis are so steeped in the love of Krishna that while others may only aspire to reach the state of oneness with the Lord, these simple cowherdesses have already attained it. Lord Krishna is construed as the quintessential romantic hero with tenderness and teasing and the beauty of his dark body, enflaming the desire of the individual soul for union with God. The Lord is revealed as a supreme lover towards whom the enraptured village girls, with whom he sported in his youth, are passionately drawn, revealed ShriNaradji in the Bhakti Sutra. Lord Krishna makes us cross a new threshold of awareness that he exists intensely in our hearts when we sing his praise and dwells in our longing for him, giving rise to kam or passion, which is pristine and pious in the earthly dialect.

His rasa, it is the nitya leela which takes place every day and eternally. Dear to Lord Krishna, Nidhi Van is a spectator of his divine play. The romantic dalliance of Shri Radha-Krishna is enacted mostly in isolated places. This playful love sport, which is both real and illusionary, making Lord Krishna human and divine at the same time, endears him and brings delight to all his bhaktas. Even today, devotees ardently believe that the divine couple visits this Van at night and all the trees present in the Nidhi van are gopis who have taken the form of a tree and together at nightfall, they do the rasa leela.

Such is the love of Krishna. Pure and delightful, just to experience something as this is enlightenment to a human. It is emergence with the divine. Maharaj ji, a great saint who resided in Vrindavan, says in one of his compositions:

"Tum nikat main nikat tam, yeh achraj ki baat nahin |"

Which means: 'It isn't astonishing that Krishna, the Supreme Lover, is near but Radha, the Beloved, is even nearer. '

According to him, devotion for the divine couple is a state of indescribable sweetness wherein there is no Radha and no Krishna, there is just RadhaKrishna. 'Main hi tum ya tum hi main' which translates to 'I am you and you are me.'

TEN

The divine knowledge

"We ought to be moved by the sorrow of mankind and suffering of creation. This is the distinctive trait of a benevolent mind."

-Shri Manohar Baba

Love, compassion, purity, devotion, we learn and absorb all of this from Krishna, but why do people say he taught dharma to the world as well? When I took the first step in this journey, it started with ignorance, ego, anger, and no idea of love whatsoever. I am still very young to comprehend a lot of things but this was a start. This is where I had to begin, and with this book, my quest does not end, rather my journey starts towards the divine couple. Whilst writing this book, I learned and experienced so much that it led me down a path I had never imagined. Bhagavat Gita , chapter 4 verse 7 :

yadāyadā hi dharmasya

glānirbhavatibhārata

abhyutthānamadharmasya

tadātmānaṁsrjāmyaham

'Whenever and wherever there is a decline in religious practice, O descendant of Bharata, and a predominant rise of irreligion—at that time I descend Myself.'

Krishna, along with his romantic dalliances, came on earth to teach dharma to rid the earth of evil. Lord Krishna reveals the nature of time and duty to Arjuna on the field of Kurukshetra, as told in the Bhagavad Gita. The pinnacle of Krishna's strength was tested in the Mahabharata war, which deals with practical questions of politics and battle. The Pandavas and Kauravas were cousins who had been torn apart by politics. The five Pandavas, their mother, and wife Draupadi had lived in exile in a forest, cheated by their uncle. When they returned after exile to ask for a small piece of land to rule over, they were denied. This led to a nationwide battle fought in Kurukshetra. Arjuna, on behalf of the Pandavas, chose to have Krishna on their side, while

Duryodhana leader of the Kauravas, opted for his army. The main purpose of the Lord's incarnation, lucidly explained in the 'Bhagwad Gita' is for the salvation of saints, destruction of evil, and installation of righteousness. Towards the end of the Dwapar Era, atrocities were on the rise, religion had become a mere farce and all deities were in great pain.

It was during the war that Arjuna broke down, unable to fight his own brothers any longer. He asked Krishna how he could possibly kill his own relatives. Precisely then, Krishna assumed his true cosmic form.

Krishna said that dharma was supreme and we, as humans, could control only our karma or actions and not its consequences. He said that whenever there would be excess of adharma or unrighteousness, he would take birth to rid the world of evil. He endorses that only those who sincerely worship Him and come to Him alone for protection would attain *moksha* or salvation. During this Mahabharata war, Krishna explained various matters to Arjun, which was later on compiled as the Bhagavat Gita, or the song of god.

The Bhagavad Gita is a spiritual discourse delivered by Krishna when Arjun lost his calm in the middle of the battlefield on seeing his cousins and uncles. Arjun got tied due to his worldly relations, and then Krishna narrated the Gita. The song of God talks about various subjects, namely nature of the self, need for restraint, yoga, reincarnation of souls, liberation, and so on. It contains eighteen chapters and seven hundred verses, which basically sum up life.

The Bhagavad Gita encourages us to perform our obligatory duties as a sacrificial offering to God and not to turn our back upon them. It explains how delusion arises and how we become bound to our present conditions, suggesting the various alternatives that are available to us to escape from them. An ignorant individual will just see the Bhagavat Gita from a very superficial point of view, looking at it from a religious point of view, but this book is spiritual and it severs our connection to worldly pleasures. This book also talks about jnanayoga (the path of knowledge), karmayoga (the path of action) and karma sanyasa yoga (the path of renunciation). Through practicing the path of knowledge, one gains an insight into inner self and becomes aware of salvation and the importance of achieving it. Practicing karma yoga, the path of action, one fulfills the obligatory duties to family and society as an offering to Krishna. Once a person realizes the inner self, gains knowledge, and completes his duties to the society, it is then karma sanyasa yoga, and renunciation happens as a realization of attachments takes place. It is not actions but attachment to the results of his actions which is responsible for worldly bondage. When a seeker practices these different types of yoga for a considerable time, he develops sattva or purity and divine qualities which are enumerated in the Bhagavad Gita. With these refinements in his lower self or the outer consciousness, he eventually comes to the fourth and the final stage, which make him fit for the practice of bhakti yoga, or the yoga of devotion. In this stage, he experiences intense devotion and unconditional love for God.

True devotion, in which all sense of egoism dissolves and only the thought of God remains, is a product of years of practice and self-discipline. It is possible only for those who are able to restrain their senses, stabilize their minds, cultivate purity, and perform their obligatory duties in the midst of the society and their families.

The Bhagavadgita has been interpreted in many ways from ancient times, by scholars belonging to various religious traditions. The first verse in the Bhagavad Gita is

dhṛtarāṣṭrauvāca

dharma-kṣetrekuru-kṣetre

samavetāyuyutsavaḥ

māmakāḥpāṇḍavāścaiva

kimakurvatasañjaya

'Dhṛtarāṣṭra said: O Sañjaya, after assembling in the place of pilgrimage at Kurukṣhetra, what did my sons and the sons of Pāṇḍu do, being desirous to fight?' Dhritrashtra, the father of the Kauravas, asked this question in the hope that the holy land of Kurukshetra, also known as Dharamshetra, would change the mind of his vicious sons. He hoped that being in the presence of Krishna would change the situation.

Through Bhagavad Gita, Krishna educates us on the topic of soul, how we mourn the loss of a loved one whereas the soul of the loved one is still present.

dehino 'sminyathādehe

kaumāraṁyauvanaṁjarā

tathādehāntara-prāptir

dhīrastatranamuhyati

'As the embodied soul continually passes, in this body, from boyhood to youth and to old age, the soul similarly passes into another body at death. The self-realized soul is not bewildered by such a change.'

All of us have experienced fear, judgment, anger, blame, resentment, jealousy, and loneliness at some point of our lives. Once we have gone through the suffering of hurting others and inflicting pain on ourselves, it seems that there is no way out. Let's share each other's grief and be less judgmental, forgiving easily. Raising our level of consciousness will bring us to love all living beings and creation. That is what Papa used to say. This spiritual elevation not only brings about oneness but love as well, which is Krishna's Consciousness. The zenith of love can be attained only by connecting with Krishna.

Love, when directed towards the Absolute, reveals the connectedness of all of existence. Prema is what connects the soul with the whole in an eternal bond of ecstatic love.

Going back to the Supreme Lover Krishna means to reach life's ultimate goal; the return of the Self to its permanent home in Golok, where the Supreme Lover-Krishna and His Beloved Radha dwell forever.

Krishna explains that happiness and sadness are all dependent on our self, it is us who decide what matter affects us. It is us who determine how entangled we are among the worldly pleasures and it is us and only us who lament for a loss, as we are so affected by everything happening around us. It is us who have to choose the path of salvation for ourselves in the end as it is the only escape from the cycle of death and rebirth. Humans often develop a sense of attachment and from this attachment, lust takes birth, and from this, anger. Anger results in a person being delusional, which leads to bewilderment. We lose our knowledge, our intelligence and we end up egoistic and full of worldly matters.

We are always surrounded by doubts of 'to do or not to do, to be or not to be.' This book that begins with the dilemma of Arjun, urges him to make the right decision, to make a choice, and to understand. Krishna encourages Arjun to let go of confusions and dilemma, let go of pain and misery and make him understand that he is much more powerful than the problems he is facing at the moment. Similarly, the things, the challenges we face do not define us, they do not decide our life but the choices we make do, and that will be with us. Gita gives us the power understanding of how to tolerate the ups and downs in life and still carry on with our karma(work) because that is the principle of life. We have to leave our false ego and our desires to understand the basic essence of our life. Gita teaches us about our mind and how it can be a friend as well as an enemy depending upon our choices. If we befriend our mind, it stays in our control whereas as if we let our mind take control over us we get pushed over to demonic activities. There is no significant problem in our life which cannot be referred to the Bhagvad Gita for a perfect solution. Gita is not philosophy, theology, metaphysics, or poetry, but it is a practical manual for daily living in any age. Shri Krishna's message is as valid today as it was centuries ago, and it will continue tomorrow, for it describes the eternal truth of life that the fiercest battle we must wage is against all that is selfish, self-willed, and separate in us.

"When doubts haunt me, when disappointments stare me in the face, and I see not one ray of hope on the horizon, I turn to Bhagvad Gita and find a verse to comfort me; and I immediately begin to smile in the midst of overwhelming sorrow. Those who meditate on the Gita will derive fresh joy and new meanings from it every day". --**Mahatma Gandhi**

One who understands the transcendental nature of Krishna does not take birth in this material nature. Only a person who is surrounded with misery and material desires takes birth on this material planet as those who are devotees do not find joy in the worldly desires, as they have a beginning and an end whereas Krishna is eternal.

For both the *bhakta* and the *rasika*, *madhurya* is the key to understanding and celebrating the love of Radha and Krishna and in doing so, get a glimpse of one's transcendent self. As *madhurya* translates into *ananda* comes the realization that everyone is ultimately a *nayika* searching for Krishna and worshippers come to find the god within themselves. At the very end, one comes to the realization of life, which is based upon love, a very strong yet sweet emotion, an emotion that completes Krishna. For the emotion makes Krishna whole. It makes the two identities we know separately one. Radha and Krishna become RadhaKrishna

As Krishna says:

rāja-vidyārāja-guhyaṁ

pavitramidamuttamam

pratyakṣāvagamaṁdharmyaṁ

su-sukhaṁkartumavyayam

'This knowledge is the king of education, the most secret of all secrets. It is the purest knowledge, and because it gives direct perception of the self by realization, it is the perfection of religion. It is everlasting, and it is joyfully performed.'

My path was paved by my father way before I realized. With the passage of time, it started with scrolling through certain emails (to groups every morning after walk) and the books Papa read like Shrimad Bhagavat and Bhagavat Mahapuran. In addition, he made sure to read about different devotees of Krishna as well. Much later, I understood that the journey which, according to me, had started recently, had actually made its way to my heart when I was just a young child.

Uncountable visits to Vrindavana, attending sankirtans, and 'Gita' readings at Iskcon had inspired me to go down this path. My father, a devotee of Krishna, passed down the immense knowledge he had gathered to me. Sometimes, we do not understand the reasons behind certain incidents taking place in our life. However, it is Krishna who reveals religious rapture to us in the course of time.

Starting off as a kid by reading the Bhagavad Gita to writing this book, which drew me closer to Shri Radha-Krishna has been the most beautiful journey. It was a cruise filled with questions and answers, revelations and desires, a quest that gradually answered all my questions on love and life. Now I feel blessed as I had climbed the next rung of the spiritual ladder, an awakening that brought me close to the Supreme Lover Krishna and His Beloved Radha...

My expedition had started with ego and ignorance, with doubts weighing down my mind.

Even if my world is intact now, I can't bear the sight of someone else's world collapsing. An unparalleled sense of compassion for the human race seems to have overtaken me. Above all, I strongly feel like using my empathic tendencies for the greater good.

My story based on love and prayer tells us that spiritual practice is not just for ourselves and our own journey, but for life itself. We need to connect with all of creation. The Bhagavat Gita's wisdom and Shri Radha-Krishna's shringar rasa suggest ways in which the energy of our spiritual nature can elevate mankind. Eventually, we are reconnected with a spiritual understanding of humanity and creation.

It is Radharani who has to bless me with Krishna, for She controls the Supreme Lover with Her love, and perfect spiritual life is unattainable without Her grace.

Gita is the essence of life, it is the truth of life and it is the answer to all questions as well. I did start my journey with this book and with this book I am ending my book.

This is the beginning of my journey to the divine, my eternal bliss.

Epilogue

As I carried on with my life, I left a part of me on the banks of Yamuna and somewhere in the streets of Barsana. With a smirk on my face, something inside of me had already changed.

I carried on my journey towards the Adi.

CPSIA information can be obtained
at www.ICGtesting.com
Printed in the USA
LVHW032026261022
731646LV00025B/498

9 789356 285613